D0260689

Some Other Books by Purple Ronnie

Purple Ronnie's History of the World

☆

Love Poems by Purple Ronnie

☆

Purple Ronnie's Little Guide to Men

☆

Purple Ronnie's Little Guide to Girls

☆

Purple Ronnie's Little Guide for Lovers

☆

Purple Ronnie's Little Guide to Boyfriends

☆

Purple Ronnie's Little Guide for Friends

☆

Purple Ronnie's Little Book of Willies and Bottoms

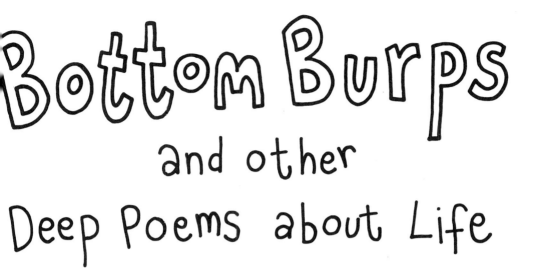

Bottom Burps
and other
Deep Poems about Life

by Purple Ronnie

First published 2000 by Boxtree
an imprint of Macmillan Publishers Ltd
25 Eccleston Place London SW1W 9NF
Basingstoke and Oxford

www.macmillan.co.uk

Associated companies throughout the world

ISBN 0 7522 7242 X

9 8 7 6 5 4 3 2

A CIP catalogue record for this book is
available from the British Library

Text by Giles Andreae
Illustrations by Janet Cronin
Printed and bound in Great Britain by The Bath Press, Bath

Contents

Part 1

Our Bodies
and the
Things They Do

love handles → ⟨ prod
⟨⟨ wobble

pose

giant
one ←

yeah!

a poem about
↓

Willies

Some people's willies are bendy
and long

And some people's willies are hairy

Some people's willies are simply
too small

But some are so huge that it's
scary

a poem about

↓

Front Bottoms

There are plenty of names for a man's private parts

But one thing that I think is rotten

Is nobody ever can seem to agree

On the name for a lady's front bottom

a poem about ↓

Spots

There's nothing wrong with
having spots
In fact it's a wonderful feeling
When you line up a ripe one
Concentrate hard
And squeeze till it splats
on the ceiling

a poem about Big Bellies

I like it when people have bellies
That are lovely and cuddly to squeeze
But not great big wobbly jellies
That dangle right down to their knees

a poem about being a
↓

Rock Star

Sometimes I dream I'm a rock
                        star
With masses of money and
                        cars
Then millions of girlies would
            scream out my name
And throw me their pants and
                their bras

a poem about ↓

Slobbing Around

There's nothing I love
More than slobbing around
And stuffing food into my belly
Like ice-cream and chocolate
        and masses of crisps
While watching fab soaps on
            the telly

a poem about ↓

Students

Being a student is totally great
Cos you don't really have to grow up
You just go to parties
With loads of cheap booze
And then drink it until you
throw up

a poem about

Being Loaded

If I was totally loaded
I'd lie in the sun on my
yacht
And I'd spend every day
Dreaming up a new way
Of blowing the whole
bloomin' lot

a poem about
↓

Shopping

Some folks are brilliant at
telling good stories
And being all clever and funny
But I'm really splendid at
shopping all day
And spending great sackloads
of money

a poem about
↓

Drinking

Some people never stop drinking
They just keep on filling their
glass
Their face goes all smiley
and wobbly and red
And then they collapse on their
arse

smashed
↓

chuck

me and
my beer

a poem about
↓

Hangovers

I sometimes wake up in the
morning
And try to get out of my bed
But it feels like my tongue
Has been dipped in some dung
And a rhino's charged into
my head

a poem about
Getting Pissed

However much booze you've been
drinking
You just want a little bit more
Your head begins reeling
You stare at the ceiling
And then you throw up on
the floor

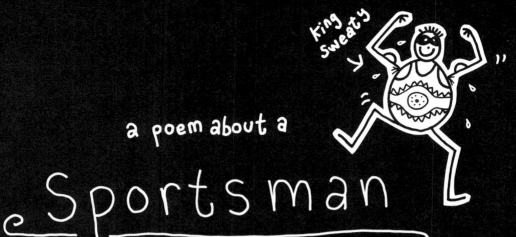

a poem about a

Sportsman

No girl can get close to a sportsman
Without passing out on the spot
The air in his room
Has the subtle perfume
Of the sweat on a wrestler's bot

a poem about

Rugby

Rugby's for people who need lots of love

Cos they hug for an hour and a half

Then take all their kit off

And sing naughty songs

And show off their bits in the bath

a poem about

Boogying

When I go out for a boogie
The girlies just can't get enough
Of the way that I wiggle
  And shimmy and jiggle
And strut out my well funky stuff

Pose

twizzle

thrust

↑ my
groovy
disco outfit

wow!
who's
he?

he's
amazing!

a poem about
↓
Football

Why do men talk about football
When most of them don't even
play?

They chant and they cheer
And swig loads of beer
And just watch it on telly
all day

a poem about

The Stars

I sometimes look up at the
stars in the sky
And it seems like the moon's
made of cheese

Somewhere I bet there's a
star made of sausage
With ketchup and hot mushy
peas

a poem about ↓

Politics

VOTE
PURPLE

If I was Prime Minister Purple
The first thing I'd do would
be this
I'd set up my very own Office
of Love
Where you'd come for a hug
or a kiss

a poem about
↓
Art

Some artists like to paint
flowers and trees
But they're not the famousest
ones
Cos most people want to see
statues of willies
And paintings of bosoms
and bums

a poem about ↓

Aliens

Some aliens hovered above me
Then beamed me up into their ship
They wired me up to their Naughty Machine
Which did groovy things to my bits

a poem about ↓

Botty Burps

Why do people's botty burps
Smell of eggs and ham?
I wish they smelt of apple pie
Or scrumptious strawberry
jam

a poem about
Letting Off

Some people get lots of pleasure

From books or from music or art
But boys seem to think it's fantastic
To just have a really good fart

a poem about a ↓

Botty Trick

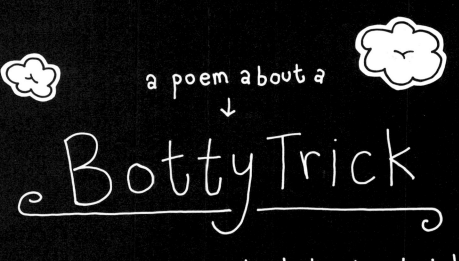

I told my friends I had a trick
They said I was a liar
So I tried to light my
                bottom burps
And set my bum on fire

a poem about ↓

Bottom Burps

Some people screw up their faces
And let out their farts bit by bit
Some people hope that they'll
creep back inside
But it's great fun to let them
just rip

a poem about
↓

Gentlemen

A gentleman loves taking ladies
for lunch

And being all fancy and proper

Then secretly sneaking to
gentlemen's clubs

Where naughty girls whip out
his whopper

a poem about ↓

Sex Goddesses

They pout at themselves in
the mirror

To get into sex goddess mode

Then wink at the boys who
walk past them

And smile as their trousers
explode

Earth Mothers

They love having baths in
rhinoceros dung

And rubbing their bosoms with
clay

It may not look pretty or
smell very nice

But it's just much more natural
that way

a poem about

Wide Boys

They're always on their mobile phones

Cutting dodgy deals

Looking sharp in shiny suits

And nifty sets of wheels

wobblers

willies

a poem about
↓

Sex Maniacs

They dream about sex every hour
of the day
They dream when they work
And they dream when they play
They dream about sex in the
bath and in bed
They never get naughty thoughts
out of their head